Dedicated to the memory of the real bus, with its charming rusted
holes and its "flighty" side door. And to all the neighborhood kids
who helped make it a jungle gym, even while it was moving.

RIP big red bus.

Special thanks to my sister for the sibling rivalry—
you'll always be number 2 in my eyes.

THIS IS A BORZOI BOOK PUBLISHED BY ALFRED A. KNOPF

Copyright © 2005 by Meghan McCarthy

All rights reserved under International and Pan-American Copyright Conventions. Published in the United
States by Alfred A. Knopf, an imprint of Random House Children's Books, a division of Random House, Inc.,
New York, and simultaneously in Canada by Random House of Canada Limited, Toronto.
Distributed by Random House, Inc., New York.

KNOPF, BORZOI BOOKS, and the colophon are registered trademarks of Random House, Inc.

www.randomhouse.com/kids

Library of Congress Cataloging-in-Publication Data
McCarthy, Meghan.
The adventures of Patty and the big red bus / by Meghan McCarthy.
p.   cm.
SUMMARY: Patty and her younger sister have exciting adventures,
from deep under the ocean to Mars, in a magical bus.
ISBN 0-375-82939-3 (trade) — ISBN 0-375-92939-8 (lib. bdg.)
[1. Adventure and adventurers—Fiction. 2. Buses—Fiction. 3. Sisters—Fiction.] I. Title.
PZ7.M1282Ad 2005
[E]—dc22   2003027389

MANUFACTURED IN MALAYSIA
March 2005   First Edition
10 9 8 7 6 5 4 3 2 1

THE ADVENTURES

OF

PATTY

AND THE

BIG RED BUS

BY MEGHAN McCARTHY

ALFRED A. KNOPF   NEW YORK

Every day I visit my bus and sometimes my sister comes along. We climb in and drive away.

Up, up, up I drive the bus . . .

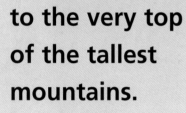

to the very top
of the tallest
mountains.

And down,
down, down . . .

to the very bottom
of the deepest oceans.

I put on my goggles
and dive in to search
for sunken treasure.
I tell my sister to stay
inside the bus where
it's safe . . .

because she can't swim
and she might drown.

Next, we drive into a big city,
full of cars and buses and taxis.
My bus speeds through the traffic . . .

just in time for me to arrive and put out a giant building fire!

I tell my sister to
wait by the bus
because she could
get burned . . .

while I save the day.

On we drive to the big-top circus.

Millions of clowns pile into my bus.
I tell my sister to get out because
she might get squished.

I drive on. My bus turns into a shiny red metal spaceship and flies high into the black sky. We soar past the stars, the sun, the planets, and even Mars!

Skillfully, I land the bus on the moon's bumpy surface.

Brave one

I tell my sister to stay inside
where it's safe while I go out
and investigate. But suddenly. . .

a giant space rock comes
flying toward me!

Luckily, it doesn't hit me.

Once I've done enough brave things,
we drive back to Earth, back to
where home is. I land the bus safely
on the ground just where it was before.
And that's where my bus sits . . .

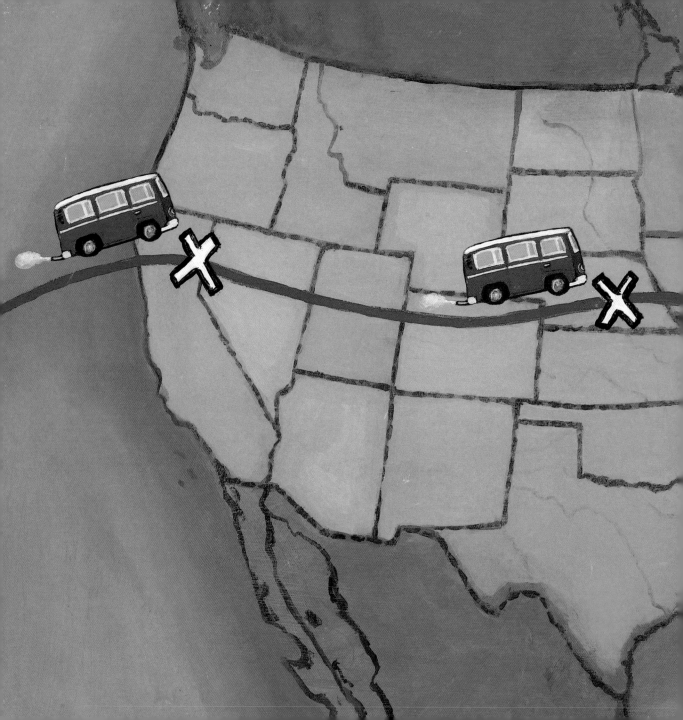